Buck Wilder's™
Adventures

Book #1

WHO STOLE THE ANIMAL POOP?

Mackinac Island Press

for the love of reading

Other Buck Wilder Books

Buck Wilder's Animal Adventures #1: Who Stole the Animal Poop?
Written by Timothy R. Smith

Library of Congress Cataloging-in-Publication Data

Smith, Tim.
   Who stole the animal poop? / written by Tim Smith.
      p. cm. -- (Buck Wilder's animal adventures ; #1)
   Summary: When someone starts removing animal droppings and
   sweeping away forest trails, making it hard for the animals to find
   their way home or know who has visited them, Buck Wilder and
   his friends investigate who is responsible, and why.
    ISBN-13: 978-1-934133-05-7 (pbk. : alk. paper)
    ISBN-10: 1-934133-05-1 (pbk. : alk. paper)
    [1. Forest animals--Fiction. 2. Forest ecology--Fiction.
   3. Ecology--Fiction. 4. Mystery and detective stories.]   I. Title.
   PZ7.S65952Who 2006
   [E]--dc22

                                        2006023858

ISBN 978-1-934133-05-7

Fiction
10 9 8 7 6 5 4 3

A Mackinac Island Press, Inc. publication
Traverse City, Michigan

www.mackinacislandpress.com

Printed in the United States

"All things are connected"

B.W.

WHO STOLE THE ANIMAL POOP?

CHAPTERS

INTRODUCTION

Deep in the forest, almost in the very center of it, lives a very nice and wise old man. He is tall and gentle, and really not as old as people think he is. He just looks older. He lives in the most awesome house you've ever seen. It's in the trees. It's a tree house and it looks kind of like this:

In this most awesome tree house lives this most awesome wise man by the name of Buck Wilder. He looks kind of like this:

Everyone thinks Buck Wilder is real smart and knows all the answers. The truth is Buck Wilder doesn't know all the answers, but he can always help you find the answers.

He has a bunch of friends–a whole lot of them. They are his animal friends and they kind of look like this:

His very best friend is Rascal Raccoon. He is always getting into things, but has a lot of good common sense and can always be trusted. In friendship trust is very important.

Rascal Raccoon looks kind of like this:

So, come and join us and we will take you on one of Buck Wilder's greatest adventures, the time someone . . . stole

    the

        animal

            poop!

TURN
THE PAGE
and
let's get started

17

CHAPTER 1

IT STARTED LIKE THIS

One day Buck Wilder was sitting around in his tree house living room being just a normal guy, eating potato chips, cleaning his fishing equipment,

and writing down stories about his life.

His good friend Rascal Raccoon was doing what he enjoyed most, taking long naps and then trying to catch fish in the aquarium.

All of a sudden the bell rang. When the bell rings it means there is a visitor at the tree house and the ladder needs to be lowered to let them in.

It is a cool ladder.

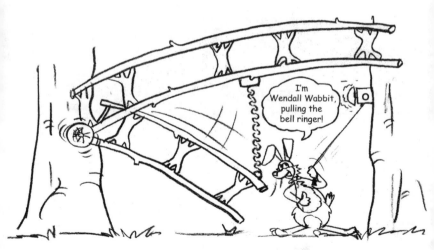

"Hello down there," yelled Rascal. "Come on up!" In two leaps and a bound there stood Wendall Rabbit.

If you knew Wendall Rabbit well, or if you saw him a lot and you tried to say his name a few times in a row, it would sound like 'Wendall Wabbit.'

So all of his animal friends, including Buck Wilder, called him Wendall Wabbit.

Say Wendall Rabbit three times fast!

"Yo, Buck," said Wendall.

"Hello, Wendall Wabbit!

"Welcome to our tree house," said Buck. "Would you like a carrot? I have some fresh lettuce too." Buck knew that rabbits were always hungry and loved to eat anything that grew in a garden.

"Thanks, Buck. A carrot sounds great, but I'm not here just to visit. I've got a problem and I need your help. Actually, all of the animals in the woods need your help. It's a big problem!"

"Okay," said Buck. "What is it?"

"Well, this one is really hard to explain. It's really strange!"

CHAPTER 2

A PROBLEM IN THE WOODS

There stood Wendall Wabbit, thumping his hind leg on the floor having a hard time explaining, so he just blurted it out. "Someone is stealing our poop!! You know—our animal droppings, our poop! I'm not kidding! Someone is actually stealing all the poop from the forest floor…and all of our tracks are gone too!"

"Oooooo," said Buck, "that is serious!"

"It sure is," said Wendall. "With all of the tracks and poops gone I can't find my friends in the woods. I don't know where they are. Their smell and footprints are gone! I can't even find my way home. All the animals are getting lost!"

"I see," said Buck. "I wonder why someone would do such a thing. Your poop and your foot tracks are your natural trail. That is how nature works.

"Rascal, this is a job for you. You are the detective and good at finding out what is going on and all the animals are your friends. Go and see what you can find out." So off went Wendall Wabbit and Rascal.

CHAPTER 3

SWEPT CLEAN

"This place is clean. There is nothing on the forest floor except a few twigs and branches. It looks like the ground has been swept clean!" said Rascal.

Hey, are the pioneers coming? That looks like a wagon trail movin' west!

Every good detective has a magnifying glass!

"If you look closely through my magnifying glass you'll see that the ground has been swept with a broom. Look here. These look like wheel tracks. These small animal tracks travel along with the wheel tracks. I wonder what this means? We should go tell Buck." So off they went.

CHAPTER 4

THE TRACKS AND POOP CHART

"Buck, I found out that Wendall is right. All the tracks and poops are missing. The forest floor has been swept clean and the

No rollerblades this time!

only thing left is a funny set of wheel tracks followed by one set of small animal tracks."

"Very interesting," said Buck. "Check out the tracks and poop chart over there and tell me if any of those tracks

look like the ones you saw." The chart
looks kind of like this:

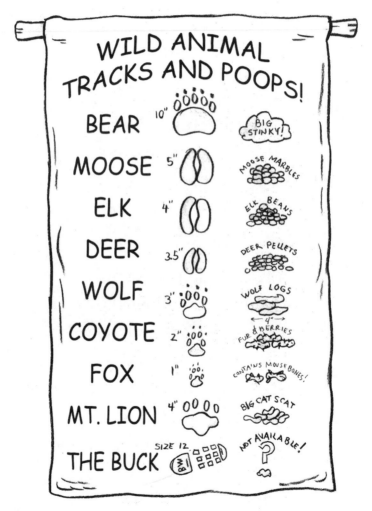

WILD ANIMAL TRACKS AND POOPS!

BEAR 10" — BIG STINKY!

MOOSE 5" — MOOSE MARBLES

ELK 4" — ELK BEANS

DEER 3.5" — DEER PELLETS

WOLF 3" — WOLF LOGS

COYOTE 2" — 4" FUR & BERRIES

FOX 1" — CONTAINS MOUSE BONES!

MT. LION 4" — BIG CAT SCAT

THE BUCK SIZE 12 — NOT AVAILABLE!

Rascal and Wendall took a good look and in no time at all figured out what kind of animal tracks they had seen. They said, "Yep, here they are. No doubt about it. Fox prints!"

"Hmmmm," said Buck. "That doesn't surprise me. Foxes are always up to something. They'll steal your chickens before you know it. Sometimes you even meet people who are sly like a fox!"

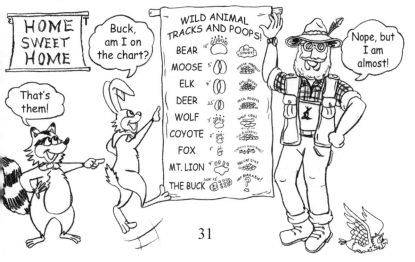

CHAPTER 5

CHECK IT OUT

"Rascal, here is what I'd like you to do. Follow those wheel tracks and see where they go. Don't be surprised if they lead directly to Sly Fox's animal den. Ask around. Get some help and see what you can find out. Then let me know what you find out," said Buck, and off they went.

Sure enough, Rascal followed the tracks right up to the front door of Sly Fox's animal den. There was a big rock rolled right in front of the opening with signs that said "KEEP OUT!!"

"I think we better tell Buck what we found," whispered Rascal, and off they went.

CHAPTER 6

NOT TOO SURPRISING

When Rascal returned he told Buck about everything he saw.

"I thought so," said Buck.

"Rascal, here is what you do. Be a lookout. You know how to climb trees. You see well in the dark, and you know how to move very quietly. Pick out a good tree next to Sly's den, climb it,

wait all night, and see what Sly Fox is up to."

So, off went Rascal. On the way he stopped to visit his friend Virgil the Owl and asked for his help to stay up all night.

Rascal knew that owls love to stay up really late, even all night, just to make their famous owl calls, "pph, ooh, whoot…whoot."

"Hi, Virgil," said Rascal. "Can you help me stay up all night?"

"I'm your man. I sure can," said Virgil. "I can see in the dark as well as you…and I love to stay up late!" So off they went.

They found a big tree next to Sly Fox's den. Rascal climbed it as Virgil flew up.

They found good lookout spots and got ready for the night.

But soon they both fell sound asleep!

CHAPTER 7

CRACK OF DAWN

Right at dawn, when the first light appears, when the black and white goes away and the color of the day starts to show, out on a nearby tree limb landed Lucy the Robin.

Lucy, like all robins, likes to get up at the first light, sing a little song, and look for breakfast.

" ♪You can't go wrong, singing a song…and say you've never heard… about the worm getting caught by the early bird ♪," sang Lucy.

Rascal and Virgil woke up right away. Both yawned, rubbed their eyes, and said, "Good morning, Lucy. You're like a morning alarm clock."

"Thanks! I like to be up early and put in a full day. Want to hear another song?" Lucy smiled.

"Thanks, Lucy–one is enough. We're awake," said Rascal sleepily.

Just then they heard more singing in the woods, and it got louder and louder as it came closer to the tree.

It was Sly Fox singing a tune and returning to his animal den.

He was wearing overalls, a wide hat, and plastic gloves. He was carrying a broom and pulling a big trash barrel. He looked tired.

" ♪ Work all night, sleep all day. Wish I had money to store away ♪," he sang. Most animals like to sing or hum a little song.

"I think we should talk to Sly," said Virgil, and down they came.

CHAPTER 8

GOOD MORNING SLY

"Good morning, Sly," said both Rascal and Virgil.

"Good morning, Rascal. Good morning, Virgil. What's up?" said Sly. "What were you doing sleeping up in that tree?"

"Oh, we weren't exactly sleeping," said Virgil. "We just took a little nap."

"We came to visit you," said Rascal. "We are trying to figure out what you are doing. Dirty overalls. Big broom. Plastic gloves. Why do you smell so bad?"

"Can you keep it a secret? You know I'm a fox and that's how I like to work–secretly!" said Sly.

"Sure," replied Rascal.

"Well, I am a clean-up man," explained Sly. "I go out into the woods at night while everyone is asleep and I have been sweeping up all of the animal poop I can find."

"What?" said Rascal in disbelief.

"I sweep up as much animal poop as I can. It is free. It just sits on the forest floor, all over the place, for anyone to pick up if they want it."

"Why would anyone ever want to pick up poop?" said Rascal. "And why would you even touch it? Eewww-www! Stinky!"

CHAPTER 9

WHAT?

"I sell it," said Sly.

"What?" said Rascal again, in more disbelief.

"It's true, I'm selling it. All I can get! I simply sweep it up, put it into bags and sell it for what people call fertilizer. They love it! They put it into their gardens, around their trees, flowers, and crops–just to help everything

grow better. I make money."

"Oh no," said Virgil. "Bags of smelly poop, yuk!"

"Sly, can we all talk with Buck? You have made a problem in the woods," said Rascal.

"No problem," said Sly. "I am making good money and it is a really fox-like thing to do. I have my own 'Sly Fox Fertilizer Company.' I hope to have a bigger fox den, a bigger TV, and have my chickens delivered!"

"That's really good, Sly, but I still think we need to talk with Buck."

"Okay," said Sly reluctantly. "Let's go." And off they went.

CHAPTER 10

EXPLANATION

So Sly explained what he was up to and Rascal explained what he saw and Buck just listened carefully.

Then Buck said, "Sly, how about a bowl of homemade chicken soup?"

"I'd love it," said Sly. "I've been up working all night. I'm tired and hungry. Sounds great. Thanks, Buck."

So Rascal, Buck, and Sly sat down

to some homemade chicken soup.

"Sly, do you mind taking off those work clothes. They kind of smell. Poop is stinky," Buck said.

"No problem," said Sly as he eagerly ate his soup.

"I admire your hard work, but I think you are creating a big problem," Buck said. "Let me explain.

"First, your broom is erasing all

the tracks on the forest floor. Animals use those tracks to find their way home, to see where their friends went, or who came to visit. They are the real animal roads in the woods.

"More important, you are sweeping up the natural fertilizer from our forest floor that all the trees, plants, and flowers need here.

"They also need that nourishment to grow, smile, and be happy. It's the natural way they live. They can't live on water alone. You see, all things are connected."

"Wow, Buck," said Sly. "I never thought of that. I would never mean any harm to the woods or to any of my friends. Oh, I feel a little bad now.

Thanks, Buck. I needed to know that.

"I'll stop sweeping and collecting animal poop, and, to be truthful, it was pretty smelly work and I had to be up all night.

"The 'Sly Fox Fertilizer Company' is now closed. Being a fox, I have a lot more fun trying to catch chickens. Thanks for the soup, Buck.

"See you later, Rascal," and Sly Fox went back to the woods.

CHAPTER 11

BACK TO NORMAL

In a short period of time everything went back to normal. The poop was back. The footprints were back. The animals found their way home, no one got lost, and all the trees, plants, and flowers had big smiles on their faces.

Life in the tree house also went back to normal. Rascal took long naps and then practiced his catch and release fishing technique. Buck went fishing as often as he could and continued to write more adventure stories.

It stayed very peaceful and natural for a long time until one day another big problem happened in the woods. Lucy the Robin and her twin sister Sadie came to Buck with the sad news that they couldn't sing anymore. It was a big problem in the woods and you can learn why in Buck Wilder's next adventure book, 'The Work Bees Go on Strike!' See you there!

SECRET MESSAGE DECODING PAGE

Hidden in this book is a secret Buck Wilder message. You need to figure it out. Hidden in many of the drawings are letters that, when put together, make up a statement, a Buck Wilder statement. Your job is to find those letters and always remember the message – it's important.

DO NOT write in this book if it's from the library, your classroom, or borrowed from someone.

If you need help finding the hidden letters turn the page.

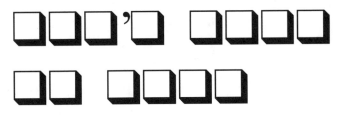

14 letters make up 4 words.

The secret letters are hidden on the following pages in this order…

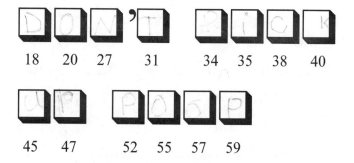

| 18 | 20 | 27 | 31 | | 34 | 35 | 38 | 40 |

| 45 | 47 | | 52 | 55 | 57 | 59 |

14 letters make up 4 words.

Remember – Don't Write in this Book!

for the love of reading